Rollerblading Royals

Rollerblading Royals

KAREN WALLACE AND RUSSELL AYTO

Hodder
Children's
Books

a division of Hodder Headline plc

To Pat with love

Chapter One

King Clements didn't like
fancy stuff like caviar and
champagne.

10

He didn't like living in a
huge castle with fabulous
views.

And he hated wearing furry collars and a crown encrusted with gold and diamonds.

King Clements just wanted to be like everybody else.

One day a circus came to town.

King Clements summoned
his servants.

"Bring me the royal
dressing-up box," he cried.
"Everyone else is going to the
circus. I shall go in disguise."

14

The servants were
horrified.

"What happens if the
Queen finds out?" they asked.

15

"A Queen's place is in her castle," replied King Clements.

Then he climbed into a baggy clown suit and strode out of the door.

Chapter Two

Queen Clementina sat in her bedroom feeling bored as usual.

Queen Clementina's bedroom looked like a movie star's dressing room.

Except that there was a
rollerblading track around the
floor. And the walls were
covered with posters of
rollerblading champions.

The sound of the circus
floated up through the
window.

It was the
loveliest sound
Queen Clementina
had ever heard.

20

She summoned her
servants.

"Bring me the royal dressing-up box," she cried.
"Everyone else is going to the
circus. I shall go in disguise."
The servants were
horrified.

"What happens if the King finds out?" they asked.

"A King's place is in his castle," replied Queen

Clementina as she squeezed into something skimpy covered in sequins.

Then she strapped on her rollerblades and shot out of the room.

Chapter Three

In a caravan behind the lion's cage, Kevin, the King of Clowns, stared at himself in the mirror.

There was a big smile on his face but inside Kevin wasn't feeling happy at all.

He was fed up with being
a clown.

It was hard work.

And he was fed up with
working hard like everyone
else.

Through the window of his caravan he could just see the towers of the king's castle.

"Bet he eats caviar and champagne every day," grumbled Kevin as he pulled on his big flappy shoes. "I wouldn't mind a bit of that."

Chapter Four

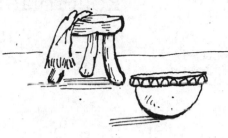

Inside her caravan, Ricky the Rollerblading Queen stared at her feet.

Her feet were in a bowl of cold water because they were very tired. They were also puffy and lumpy and bruised.

Ricky looked at a pair of dainty white rollerblades with gold tassles lying on the floor.

How on earth was she
going to squash her poor
swollen feet into those
rollerblades?

Through the window, she
could just see the towers of
the castle.

She closed her eyes.

Wouldn't it be nice to be a *real* Queen for a change?

"Excuse me," said a breathless voice. "I think you are absolutely brilliant!"

Ricky looked up.

Queen Clementina stood at her door.

"Your Majesty!" gasped Ricky.

"How did you know it was me?" asked the Queen in a disappointed voice.

"You forgot to take off your crown," said Ricky. "And why are you wearing rollerblades?"

"It's my favourite thing," replied the Queen.

She saw Ricky's fake gold and diamond crown hanging on the wall.

In fact, I would swap your crown for mine any day.

Ricky the Rollerblading Queen looked at her puffy white feet. Then she looked at her tiny white rollerblades.

It was an offer she couldn't refuse.

Queen Clementina pulled
her crown off her head.
    Ricky pulled hers off the
wall.

"It's a deal," said the
Queen.
    "It's a deal," replied Ricky.

Then she thought, Oh dear, I wonder what Kevin will say. Because Kevin, King of Clowns, was married to Ricky, the Rollerblading Queen.

Chapter Five

Kevin, King of Clowns, stared at a clown that looked just like him.

Except for one thing.

This clown was wearing a crown.

"Excuse me," said King
Clements, "I think you're
absolutely brilliant. Clowns
are my favourite thing and I
have followed your career
with great interest."

Kevin, King of Clowns
was dumbfounded.

Your Majesty!

"How did you know it
was me?" asked King
Clements in a disappointed
voice.

37

"You forgot to take off your crown," said Kevin.

"Oh *that*," said King Clements snatching the crown from his head. "I hate it."

"You do?" cried Kevin, rolling his eyes and waggling his hands in disbelief.

"I do," cried King Clements, jumping sideways and cocking his head. "In fact, I would swap my crown for your orange wig, any day."

Out of the corner of his eye,
Kevin saw the
towers of the
castle.
   He
thought
of all that
caviar and
champagne.

   It was an offer he couldn't
refuse.

King Clements held out his crown.

Kevin, King of Clowns, pulled off his wig.

"It's a deal," said the King.
"It's a deal," replied Kevin.

41

Then he thought, Oh dear,
I wonder what Ricky will say.
Because Ricky the
Rollerblading Queen had firm
views about who made the
decisions in married life.

Chapter Six

And so it happened, later that evening Kevin was surprised to meet Ricky in the great hall of the castle.

But both of them were so amazed and delighted as well as overworked and overtired, neither of them said much at all.

Instead they drank champagne and ate caviar for supper.

They looked at the fabulous views over the countryside.

Then they went to sleep in a huge feather bed.

And the next morning they didn't bother to get up for breakfast.

Because breakfast was brought up to them.

Later that evening King
Clements met Queen
Clementina in the ring.

King Clements did wonder-
ful things with plastic bones
and prancing white poodles.

He juggled plates and
made custard pies fall in all
the right places.

Queen Clementina bladed like a shooting star. She leapt, she flew and she landed light as a feather.

Some people said she was the best rollerblader they had ever seen.

At the end of the show the
audience stood on their feet
to clap and cheer.

That night the King and
Queen grabbed a sandwich
for supper and slept on bunk
beds in a caravan.

They had never worked
so hard in their lives

and they had never
felt so happy.

Chapter Seven

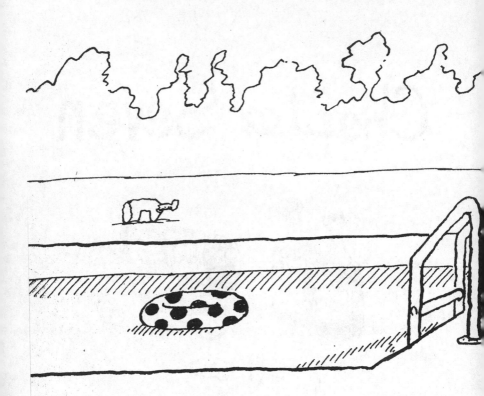

After almost a year, Ricky and
Kevin had eaten all the caviar
and champagne they could
manage. They had lounged
by swimming pools, they had
draped themselves over
velvet sofas.

52

They had
stared at the fabulous
views until their eyes
bubbled.

And they were just begin-
ning to get a teeny weeny bit
bored.

After almost a year, King Clements and Queen Clementina had toured the land.

They had performed every night.

They had eaten almost three hundred and sixty-five sandwiches each.

And they were just beginning to feel overworked and overtired like everyone else.

Chapter Eight

Exactly a year later, the circus came back to town.

King Clements was in his caravan getting ready.

There was a big smile on his face but inside he wasn't

feeling happy at all.

He couldn't stop dreaming of caviar, champagne and breakfast in bed.

At the other end of the caravan, Queen Clementina lifted her feet out of a bowl of cold water.

There was a tap on the caravan door.

Kevin, King of Clowns and Ricky the Rollerblading Queen stood outside.

"Excuse us," they said. "We've been following your careers with great interest and we think you're absolutely brilliant."

And you'll never guess what happened next!

That night and for one
night only, there were two
Clown Kings and two
Rollerblading Queens!

The audience couldn't
believe their eyes.
It was SENSATIONAL!

At the end of the show,
they clapped and cheered
and stomped their feet so
hard, that the floor collapsed
and the tent fell down.

Chapter Nine

In fact, King Clements and
Queen Clementina still talk
about it. But only when Kevin
and Ricky come to stay.

Most of the time, they are
too busy.

King Clements runs a
School for Clowns in the castle.

And Queen Clementina
teaches rollerbladers to leap
and fly and land as light
as a feather.

But when Kevin and Ricky
come to stay, they sit around
and drink champagne and eat
caviar.

And the next morning they
all have breakfast in bed!

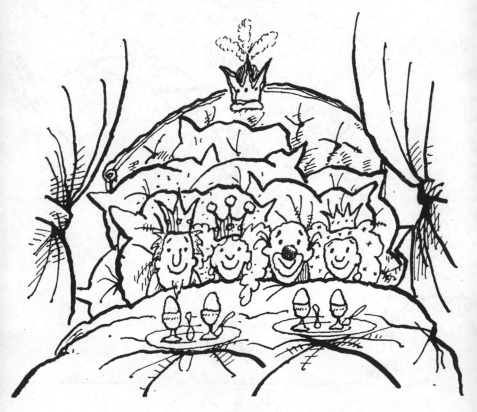